Gallup Guides for Youth Facing Persistent Prejudice

Blacks

GALLUP GUIDES FOR YOUTH FACING PERSISTENT PREJUDICE

- Asians
- Blacks
- Hispanics
- Jews
- The LGBT Community
- Muslims
- Native North American Indians
- People with Mental and Physical Challenges

GALLUP GUIDES FOR YOUTH FACING PERSISTENT PREJUDICE

Blacks

Jaime Seba

Mason Crest

Mason Crest
370 Reed Road
Broomall, Pennsylvania 19008
www.masoncrest.com

Printed and bound in the United States of America.

First printing
9 8 7 6 5 4 3 2 1

ISBN-13: 978-1-4222-2462-5 (hardcover series)
ISBN-13: 978-1-4222-2464-9 (hardcover)
ISBN-13: 978-1-4222-9337-9 (e-book)

Library of Congress Cataloging-in-Publication Data

Seba, Jaime.
 Gallup guides for youth facing persistent prejudice: Blacks / by Jaime Seba.
    p. cm.
 Includes bibliographical references and index.
 ISBN 978-1-4222-2464-9 (hardcover) -- ISBN 978-1-4222-2462-5 (series hardcover) -- ISBN 978-1-4222-9337-9 (ebook)
 1. African Americans--Juvenile literature. 2. Prejudices--Juvenile literature. 3. Racism--Juvenile literature. I. Title. II. Title: Blacks.
 E185.615.S373 2013
 305.896'073--dc23
                                    2012017111

Produced by Harding House Publishing Services, Inc.
www.hardinghousepages.com
Interior design by Micaela Sanna.
Page design elements by Cienpies Design / Illustrations | Dreamstime.com.
Cover design by Torque Advertising + Design.

CONTENTS

What Is Prejudice?

The root word of prejudice is "pre-judge." Prejudiced people often judge others based purely on their race or ethnic group; they make assumptions about others that may have no basis in reality. They believe that if your skin is darker or you speak a different language or wear different clothes or worship God in a different way, then they already know you are not as smart, not as nice, not as honest, not as valuable, or not as moral as they are. Black Americans have been the victims of prejudice since the United States was born.

Why do human beings experience prejudice? Sociologists believe humans have a basic tendency to fear anything that's unfamiliar or unknown. Someone who is strange (in that they're not like us) is scary; they're automatically dangerous or inferior. If we get to know the strangers, of course, we end up discovering that they're not so different from ourselves. They're not so frightening and threatening after all. But too often, we don't let that happen. We put up a wall between the strangers and ourselves. We're on the inside; they're

We often separate ourselves from those who are different. In many cases, this reaction is caused by fear.

Blacks

High School Stereotypes

The average high school has its share of stereotypes—lumping a certain kind of person together, ignoring all the ways that each person is unique. These stereotypes are often expressed with a single word or phrase: "jock," "nerd," "goth," "prep," or "geek." The images these words call to mind are easily recognized and understood by others. But that doesn't mean they're true!

on the outside. And then we peer over the wall, too far away from the people on the other side to see anything but our differences. That's what has often happened when whites and blacks interacted in the United States.

And here's where another human tendency comes into play: stereotyping.

STEREOTYPES

A stereotype is a fixed, commonly held idea or image of a person or group that's based on an **oversimplification** of some observed or imagined trait. Stereotypes assume that whatever

Group Pressure

Why do people continue to believe stereotypes despite evidence that may not support them? Researchers have found that it may have something to do with group pressure. During one experiment, seven members of a group were asked to state that a short line is longer than a long line. About a third of the rest of the group agreed that the short line was longer, despite evidence to the contrary. Apparently, people conform to the beliefs of those around them in order to gain group acceptance.

is believed about a group is typical for each and every individual within that group. "All blondes are dumb," is a stereotype. "Women are poor drivers," is another. "Men are slobs," is yet another, and "Gay men are **effeminate**," is one as well.

Many stereotypes tend to make us feel superior in some way to the person or group being stereotyped. Not all stereotypes are negative, however; some are positive—"Black men are good at basketball," "Gay guys have good fashion sense," or "Asian students are smart"—but that doesn't make them true.

They ignore individuals' uniqueness. They make assumptions that may or may not be accurate.

We can't help our human tendency to put people into categories. As babies, we faced a confusing world filled with an amazing variety of new things. We needed a way to make sense of it all, so one of our first steps in learning about the world around us was to sort things into separate slots in our heads: small furry things that said *meow* were kitties, while larger furry things that

Prejudice Starts Inside

Sociologists have found that people who are prejudiced toward one group of people also tend to be prejudiced toward other groups. In a study done in 1946, people were asked about their attitudes concerning a variety of ethnic groups, including Danireans, Pirraneans, and Wallonians. The study found that people who were prejudiced toward blacks and Jews also distrusted these other three groups. The catch is that Danireans, Pirraneans, and Wallonians didn't exist! This suggests that prejudice's existence may be rooted within the person who feels prejudice rather than in the group that is feared and hated.

Six Characteristics of a Racial Minority Group

1. Minority group members suffer oppression at the hands of another group.

2. A minority group is identified by certain traits that are clearly visible and obvious.

3. Minorities see themselves as belonging to a special and separate social unit; they identify with others like themselves.

4. A person does not voluntarily become a member of a minority; he or she is born into it.

5. Members of racial minority groups usually don't marry outside the group. If intermarriage is high, ethnic identities and loyalties are weakening.

6. "Minority" is a social, not a numerical concept. In other words, it doesn't matter how many members of a particular "out-group" live in a region compared to the "in-group"; what matters are who has the power and social prestige.

If these three individuals came to your high school, you would probably instantly assign them each to a stereotype!

said *arf-arf* were doggies; cars went *vroom-vroom*, but trains were longer and went *choo-choo*; little girls looked one way and little boys another; and doctors wore white coats, while police officers wore blue. These were our earliest stereotypes. They were a handy way to make sense of the world. They helped us know what to expect, so that each time we faced a new person or thing, we weren't starting all over again from scratch.

Four Characteristics of Racial Prejudice

1. a feeling of superiority
2. a feeling that the minority is different and alien
3. a feeling of rightful claim to power, privilege, and status
4. a fear and suspicion that the minority wants to take the power, privilege, and status from the dominant group

But stereotypes become dangerous when we continue to hold onto our mental images despite new evidence. (For instance, as a child you may have decided that all dogs bite—which means that when faced by friendly, harmless dogs, you assume they're dangerous and so you miss out on getting to know all dogs.) Stereotypes are particularly dangerous and destructive when they're directed at persons or groups of persons. That's when they turn into prejudice.

RACISM

Prejudice and racism go hand-in-hand. Prejudice is an attitude, a way of looking at the world. When it turns into action it's

What Does the United Nations Have to Say?

"The term 'racial discrimination' shall mean any distinction, exclusion, restriction, or preference based on race, colour, descent, or national or ethnic origin that has the purpose or effect of nullifying or impairing the recognition, enjoyment or exercise, on an equal footing, of human rights and fundamental freedoms in the political, economic, social, cultural or any other field of public life."

called discrimination. Discrimination is when people are treated differently (and unfairly) because they belong to a particular group of people. Racism is a combination of the two. It's treating members of a certain "race" differently because you think they're not as good, simply because they belong to that race. You might say that prejudice is the root of racism—and discrimination is its branches and leaves.

There's one other concept that's important to racism as well—the belief that human beings can be divided into groups that are truly separate and different from one another. Scientists aren't convinced this is really possible, though.

A lot of the time, racism is built on words that mean different things in different places. People who are classified as "black" in the United States, for example, might be considered "white" in Brazil, where "black" is defined quite differently from the way it is in America. In America, someone is a black if she has even the slightest appearance of having descended from Africans, no matter how light her skin may be or how European her features. In Brazil, on the other hand, a poor person with white skin might be called "black," simply because of her lifestyle. In South Africa, the same person might be called "colored," meaning her ancestors were both European and African.

So race really isn't something that's black and white! People are more alike than they're different, no matter what color their skin is or what continent their ancestors came from. In fact, scientists tell us that the idea of race is pretty much only useful as a medical concept—some groups of people from various parts of the world are more likely to get some illnesses than others, and some may respond better to certain medications. This has to do with the **genes** that people tend to share if their ancestors come from the same place. **Sickle cell disease**,

Ethnocentrism

Ethnocentrism refers to a tendency to view one's own ethnic group's behaviors as "normal." Other groups are not only viewed as different, but they are seen as strange and sometimes inferior.

for example, is usually found among people whose ancestors lived in Africa or the Mediterranean region. **Cystic fibrosis** is more common among people whose ancestors came from Europe. People descended from Africans don't always respond as well to certain kinds of heart medicines.

But black Americans are just as likely to be smart as white Americans. They are just as trustworthy and kind, just as moral and hardworking. Some blacks get in trouble with the law—and so do some whites. Many blacks have problems. So do many whites.

Racism tells lies. Prejudice is one of those lies.

History Lesson

Black Americans' ancestors did not come to the United States by choice. Instead, they were captured from their homes, herded at gunpoint onto ships in West Africa, and then taken across the Atlantic Ocean. Conditions on the slave ships were horrific; more than one in ten Africans died on the way, over a million and a half people. Once they arrived in the Americas, they were sold at auctions and then forced to work fifteen, sixteen, or even eighteen hours a day.

Slavery's History

The earliest human communities had no slaves. Hunter-gatherers and the earliest farmers collected or grew just enough food for themselves, so they had no use for slavery: one more pair of hands would have only meant one more mouth to feed. There was no advantage in "owning" another human being.

Once people gathered in towns and cities, however, a surplus of food created in the countryside (often on large farms) made possible the production of goods in towns. Having a reliable source of cheap labor that cost no more than the minimum of food and lodging was now a real benefit the owners of large farms and workshops. These were the conditions that gave birth to slavery. Every ancient civilization used slaves.

In the ancient world, slaves came from a variety of sources. War supplied most of them; when a town fell to a hostile army, the inhabitants who would make useful workers were taken as slaves (and the rest were killed). Pirates also offered their captives for sale. A criminal might be sentenced to slavery, and an unpaid debt could lead to slavery for the debtor. Poor people sometimes sold their own children. But slavery was never associated with racial differences. That came later.

In the 18th century, Europeans began going to Africa to capture other human beings to be used as slaves.

Africans who arrived in the British Caribbean islands in the eighteenth century had little chance of survival; 1.6 million human beings were brought there during the 1700s, but by the end of the century, there were only 600,000 living slaves. In North America, however, the more **temperate** climate and greater quantities of fresh food gave the Africans a better chance of survival. The slave population there was 500,000 at the beginning of the eighteenth century, and by 1860, it had grown to 6 million. Still, the death toll was heavy and

An Early Alternative to Slavery

At first, North American plantation owners used indentured servants instead of slaves to meet their labor needs. These individuals had signed a contract to work for three, five, or seven years for no wages in exchange for their passage across the Atlantic. In 1638, an indentured servant cost £12 while a slave cost £25.37. Since neither the servant nor the slave was likely to live more than four or five years, the servants seemed to offer the plantation owners "more bucks for their dollar" (or their pounds) than the slaves did.

This inhumanity was not based on racism. If prejudice was at play, it had more to do with the fact that merchants and those in government did not see the human value of those who were poor. At the same period of time (and for the next two centuries), "pressed" men—poor men who had been kidnapped from the streets—manned the British navy.

horrifying: 10 million Africans had crossed the Atlantic to North America, compared to only 2 million Europeans, and yet the white population was up to 12 million by the mid-1800s, twice as much as the black.

Once Europeans began the large-scale production of tobacco and sugar in their North American colonies, they needed an enormous labor force to keep their plantations thriving. White servants weren't plentiful enough to meet their needs, so plantation owners turned more and more to the African slave trade. Before long, a thriving economy had been built in North America—and slavery was the backbone that ran down its middle.

In the beginning, though, slaves and servants were treated much the same. Both could be branded with an "R" (for "runaway") if they tried to escape, and both worked alongside each other in the fields. They often lived together and spent their free time together. Sometimes they even married each other. And once in a while, they joined together to fight back against the plantation owners.

This worried the white landowners. In self-defense, they instituted laws that would divide the Africans and the poor whites. The Virginia House of Burgesses, for instance, decreed that "negro" slaves could be lashed if they got in a fight with a white servant; "negroes and mulattos" could also be killed if they tried to escape from their "masters." And any white person who married a person of color would be **banished** from the colony.

As more and people owned slaves, and slavery became essential to an entire way of life, eighteenth-century societies needed to justify their actions. This was a time when most

The economy of the Southern colonies and the Caribbean Islands came to depend on slave labor. This painting shows African slaves' role in eighteenth-century sugarcane production.

Skin Color and Racism

In the ancient and medieval worlds, people apparently did not regard skin color as any more significant than any other physical characteristic (such as height, hair color, or eye color). Tomb paintings from ancient Egypt show what looks like random mixtures of white-, brown-, and black-skinned figures. In early sixteenth-century Dutch paintings, people with white and black skins are portrayed side by side as equals.

What's more, the early slave traders and owners did not use racial inferiority to excuse slavery. Instead, they used ancient Greek and Roman writings that justified the enslavement of those captured during war. Eventually, however, this way of thinking would no longer work for the large-scale slave economy of the 1700s. People were well aware now that slaves were purchased from merchants who had captured innocent Africans. And more and more children were born and raised as slaves.

100 DOLLARS REWARD!

Ranaway from the subscriber on the **27th** of July, my Black Woman, named

EMILY,

Seventeen years of age, well grown, black color, has a whining voice. She took with her one dark calico and one blue and white dress, a red corded gingham bonnet; a white striped shawl and slippers. I will pay the above reward if taken near the Ohio river on the Kentucky side, or **THREE HUNDRED DOLLARS**, if taken in the State of Ohio, and delivered to me near Lewisburg, Mason County, Ky. **THO'S. H. WILLIAMS.**

August 4, 1853.

A poster for a runaway slave demonstrates that African Americans were considered "property," rather than human beings.

whites considered themselves Christians, so they turned to the Bible to find an excuse for slavery. Christian supporters of slavery began claiming that Africans were descended from Ham, the cursed son of Noah—and therefore, God didn't care if Africans were enslaved; in fact, He approved. Those white-skinned folk who had more scientific leanings (since the **Enlightenment** was also sweeping through Europe) used another (though similar) **justification**, namely that Africans were "sub-human." This meant the great thinkers of the century could proclaim that "all men are created equal," and still condone slavery, since non-whites were not men. Racism based on color was now born.

For most blacks taken to the Americas, life became a nightmare of cruelty and hard work. One slave said it seemed the fields stretched "from one end of the earth to the other." Everyone—men, women, children, old people, sick people—worked. On most plantations, a horn or bell woke workers at about four in the morning, and thirty minutes later, slaves were expected to be out of their cabins and on their way to the fields; anyone who was late was whipped. An ex-slave in Virginia recalled seeing women scurrying to the fields "with their shoes and stockings in their hands, and a petticoat wrapped over their shoulders, to dress in the fields the best way they could." Overseers armed with whips made sure that workers never slacked.

When the United States was born and then expanded west, the cultivation of cotton spread as well, taking slavery with it. Historian Peter Kolchin writes, "By breaking up existing families and forcing slaves to relocate far from everyone and everything they knew," this **migration** repeated many of the horrors of the Atlantic slave trade. In 1820, every child born into slavery in the South had a one in three chance of being sold to a slave trader who would resell the child out of the area where he or she had been born. Slave traders didn't care about purchasing or transporting entire slave families. As a result, families were separated from each other, and many would never see one another again.

Once they reached their destinations, the transplanted people faced a new life that was no better than the old one. Clearing trees and planting crops on unplowed fields was backbreaking work. Food was scarce, mosquitoes were plentiful, and people were exhausted. No wonder then that the death rate made some planters prefer to rent slaves rather than own them!

An Arkansas slaveholder wrote:

Now, I speak what I know, when I say it is like "casting pearls before swine" to try to persuade a negro to work. He must be made to work, and should always be given to understand that if he fails to perform his duty he will be punished for it.

Violence was the method used to control these human beings. According to one plantation overseer:

negroes are determined never to let a white man whip them and will resist you, when you attempt it; of course you must kill them in that case.

Under the law, these human beings were not considered to be persons—unless they committed crimes. An Alabama court made this contradictory statement, that slaves

are rational beings, they are capable of committing crimes; and in reference to acts which are crimes, are regarded as persons. Because they are slaves, they are incapable of performing civil acts, and, in reference to all such, they are things, not persons.

The economic value of plantation slavery grew even greater in 1793 when Eli Whitney invented the cotton gin, a device designed to separate cotton fibers from the seedpods. The invention meant the amount of cotton processed in a day increased by fifty times. Factories needed more cotton—and plantation owners needed more slaves to produce it.

Just as the demand for slaves was increasing, however, the U.S. Constitution reduced the supply by banning further **importation** of slaves. Any new slaves would have to be descendants of ones currently in the United States.

Not everyone in the United States was comfortable with the concept of slave labor. Beginning in the 1750s, more and more people began to push for the **abolition** of slavery. All the Northern states passed **emancipation** acts between 1780 and 1804, and the movement to end slavery grew stronger. In 1830, William Lloyd Garrison led a religious movement that declared slavery to be a personal sin from which slave owners should repent.

The American Civil War, which began in 1861, eventually brought an end to slavery in the United States. In 1863, President Abraham Lincoln's Emancipation Proclamation promised freedom to all slaves in the Southern Confederacy.

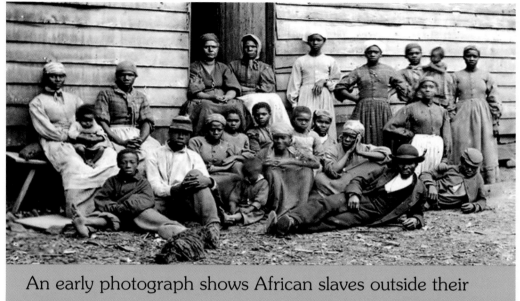

An early photograph shows African slaves outside their dwelling.

According to the Census of 1860, this policy freed nearly four million slaves (once the South was once more under the Union's control), more than 12 percent of the total population of the United States.

After the war, slavery was illegal throughout the United States—but that didn't mean that black Americans could take their place as the equals of white Americans. Black Americans had fewer educational, employment, and housing opportunities than whites. In the South especially, many whites found ways to maintain control over the black population.

Trying to Justify Slavery

"There are few, I believe, in this enlightened age, who will not acknowledge that slavery as an institution is a moral and political evil. It is idle to expatiate on its disadvantages. I think it is a greater evil to the white than to the colored race. While my feelings are strongly enlisted in behalf of the latter, my sympathies are more deeply engaged for the former. The blacks are immeasurably better off here than in Africa, morally, physically, and socially. The painful discipline they are undergoing is necessary for their further instruction as a race, and will prepare them, I hope, for better things. How long their servitude may be necessary is known and ordered by a merciful Providence."

—Robert E. Lee, General of the Confederate Forces

In the 1960s, the Civil Rights Movement began. Black Americans—and white Americans too—worked hard for the rights of all people. People like Martin Luther King Jr., Rosa Parks, and Thurgood Marshall spoke out and took action. The Civil Rights Movement changed American laws—and it changed the way people think as well.

But prejudice against black Americans did not go away altogether. Neither did discrimination. As a group, black Americans still did not have the same opportunities white Americans did. More blacks than whites were still poor.

Slavery had tried to erase the humanity of entire group of people. Slavery's roots are still there, deep in America's history—and long after the ugly tree was chopped down, its fruits still poison American society. Prejudice is one of these fruits.

A Real-Life Story

Wilhelmina Brown knows about prejudice. She's a black woman who grew up in the American South during the 1960s. She remembers what it was like to have to use a different restroom from white people, how it felt to see a sign that said you had to use a different drinking fountain, how much she wanted to go to the "good" beach in Myrtle Beach, South Carolina, and how she didn't understand when her parents explained that she and her family could only go to a dirty beach with dangerous currents.

"When you're a little girl," she said, "living in a big family where everyone loves you, you grow up thinking you're pretty special. You know you're pretty and smart and good with words and all that. And then one day, you go out and run smack into this completely different viewpoint. You find out that there's this whole world out there that thinks you're ugly and stupid and not as good at anything, simply because your skin is black and your ancestors came from Africa. It's a big shock."

Today, Wilhelmina wears a dark gray suit and black high-heeled shoes. She looks like she might be a lawyer. She carries her shoulders back and her head high; you can see the pride and dignity in her face. But when she tells her story, you can also hear the lingering shame and resentment of racism. Wilhelmina is a well-educated woman with a respected job—but she remembers all too well what it was like to be poor and black.

"My father was a share farmer," she says. "He worked the land for a white man, and he got to keep a share from the crops he grew. It wasn't like we ever had much money, but when I was a little thing, I never knew we were poor either. We had plenty to eat, my mama loved my daddy, we were always laughing. My parents were good people, churchgoers their whole life. They taught us kids right from wrong. They taught us to always do our best, to take pride in who we are, to be kind to other folk, to do what we could to help others who were less fortunate. So I had a happy childhood.

"The only really bad thing that happened was my uncle's death. I was a bitty thing, maybe five or six, when he died. The grownups wouldn't talk about it around us kids, but they were talking in whispers all the time, shutting the doors on us, looking sad and scared. I thought Uncle Daniel must have gotten sick and died. But then one of my older cousins told me what had really happened. He'd been hung on a rope from a tree in his front yard. The Klan had done it. Because Daniel had gotten mad and made trouble with his boss, a white man that ran everything in town.

"Well, I didn't know who or what the Klan was, so of course, my cousin explained that to me as well. It was like the worst ghost story I'd ever heard—white-robed monsters with pointed hats sneaking around in the dark, killing good people—except my cousin was saying they were *real*, not make-believe. I had nightmares for years.

"It's hard to explain to a white person what it's like growing up black. It's not like I've ever seen the Ku Klux Klan for myself. It's not like anyone ever hit me or spit on me, and I only recall

The Ku Klux Klan

Hoping to restore white supremacy, veterans of the Confederate Army founded the first Ku Klux Klan (KKK) in 1866 in the aftermath of the American Civil War. The Klan resisted Reconstruction by intimidating the newly freed black Americans and their supporters. The KKK's methods grew increasingly violent, even murderous, and eventually, federal troops moved into the South to control the Klan. The organization declined in power, and President Ulysses S. Grant destroyed it by prosecuting its members under the Civil Rights Act of 1871.

But the Klan did not remain dead. After World War I, waves of immigrants from Southern and Eastern Europe swept into America. Blacks from the South were moving to the North—and at the same time, white veterans from the war were trying to reenter the work force. Out of this tension, the second KKK rose up preaching racism, anti-Catholicism, anti-Communism, and anti-Semitism. Lynchings and other forms of violent intimidation once more became common, especially in the South. This second Klan was a formal fraternal organization, with a national and state structure. At its peak in the mid-1920s, the organization included between 4 and 5 million men.

This Klan also fell from favor during the Great Depression, and membership fell even more during World War II. But like a monster in a horror movie, the Klan refuses to remain in its grave. Independent groups opposing the Civil Rights Movement and desegregation used the Klan's name in the 1950s and 1960s. During this period, the Klan even formed alliances with Southern police departments and local governments.

Today, researchers estimate America has more than 150 Klan chapters, with 5,000 to 8,000 members. The U.S. government classifies the KKK as a hate group, a term used to describe any organization that aggressively and systematically dehumanizes members of a particular group.

that I've been called 'nigger' once in my entire life. (But you'd better believe I've never forgotten it!) And yet, it's this thing you carry with you all the time. I think it's a little like trying to explain to a man what it's like being a woman. You may have been loved and well-treated by the men in your life, treated kind and never beat or abused—but at the same time, it's this knowledge you always carry with you, this invisible thing inside your head: you can't do all the things a man can do. There's just no point trying. And it's your job to put up with men's nonsense, to smile and work hard, and not complain. Well, being black is a little like that.

"It's knowing your own parents talk different when white folks are around. These people you respect more than any other in the world, these wise, wonderful parents, they don't respect

The Ku Klux Klan claims to be a patriotic, Christian organization. In reality, it is a group built on a terrible foundation of prejudice and hatred.

themselves so much when they're around white people. So you learn that, growing up. You understand that you and all the people who look like you, all the people where you go to church, all your friends, all the grownups who love you, all of them will never have the same sort of jobs or make as much money or be as respected as the white people in the world.

"'You're as smart as a whip,' my mama always told me. 'You make up your mind right now, you're going to college.' So I did. I got a scholarship and I went to college, and I became a social worker. I grew up and I moved up North. I worked hard, and I'm good at my job. By the time I was thirty, I was the supervisor of my department, with four white women and two white men working under me. It felt so good, let me tell you!

"What hurt was when I'd go back home to South Carolina. 'You're an Oreo, girl,' my big brother told me. He meant I looked black on the outside, but I was white on the inside. He said I talked like a white woman. That made me mad. And then I noticed myself acting different when I'd go to the store or when I'd run into the people who owned my daddy's farm. I'd lower my eyes and speak soft, I'd hold my whole body different from what I would have done up in Rochester, New York, where I lived.

"Racism is an ugly, ugly thing. I've been lucky and blessed my whole life. And I'm grateful. But don't tell me racism isn't real. Or that it doesn't hurt people. I work with people every day who are angry and hopeless, who have given up, who are buried so deep in what racism has done to this country

The way to stop racism is for individuals to take a stand against it. This woman is taking part in a protest held in Calgary in Alberta, Canada, in 2007.

that they don't even know how to begin to get out. And all I can do is pass out Band-Aids most days. I tell myself that you never know what a little thing can do to bring about change in a person's life. I convince myself most of the time that I'm making a difference. But some days I get discouraged.

"The world is changing. The laws are better. People's minds are opener. But then you run into something that takes you by surprise. Like a white man I really respect telling me a young boy we've been working with is 'just like the rest of them.' He apologized, he seemed to think I'd feel better when he said, 'Wilhelmina, I never think of you as black.' Something like that makes you realize—racism is still there, hiding inside people. It's hiding inside me too, at the back of my head, making me believe I'm not quite as good as white folk. But I refuse to listen to that voice.

"So I guess that's what I'd tell young people. Don't be surprised if you find racism sneaking into your head, and don't think worse of yourself if it does. None of us can help absorbing the attitudes around us. But pay attention when that happens. Notice when racism is there in you. Call it by name. And then refuse to act on it. Tie it up and throw it away. Don't teach it to your children. Make the next generation free."

Fighting Prejudice

The United States used to be called a melting pot. This expression meant that people of different races, religions, and ethnic backgrounds had all come together in America. Today, many people think that "melting pot" is the wrong **metaphor** to use for the United States, because it implies that all these different kinds of people cooked down into a single "stew," losing their individual characteristics. Nowadays, people speak instead of the United States as a salad bowl or a mosaic—something where all the separate pieces hold on to what makes them different and special, and yet all of them contribute to something bigger, the thing that makes America what it is today.

Americans, no matter their backgrounds, share some very important beliefs. They believe in democracy, in freedom of speech, and in the right for a person to worship as he chooses. These common beliefs give us an important foundation on which to come together. They give us something to work toward, despite our differences.

President Woodrow Wilson once said that America is not set apart from other countries "so much by its wealth and power as by the fact that it was born with an **ideal**, a purpose." The United States was created to be a nation where the people rule themselves, where everyone has certain rights, regardless of the color of their skin, their religion, their gender, or how much money they have.

AMERICA'S BATTLE AGAINST PREJUDICE

At the very beginning of the United States, when the thirteen original colonies first declared their independence from England on July 4, 1776, they stated that all "are created equal, that they are endowed by their Creator with certain **unalienable** rights, that among them are Life, Liberty, and the pursuit of happiness."

America's history is the story of how it has struggled to live up to these ideals. The Civil War was a part of that struggle. Near the end of that war, President Abraham Lincoln expressed his belief in the nation's central ideal of freedom for all: "It is not merely for today, but for all time to come. . . . The nation is worth fighting for, to secure such an inestimable jewel."

This poster celebrates many of the new freedoms black Americans experienced after the Civil War, including the right to vote, and the right to an education and to be legally married, both of which had been denied them before.

In 1865, the 13th Amendment did away with slavery, but it did not give full equality to black Americans. A year later, however, the Civil Rights Act won another small victory in the battle against prejudice, stating that "all persons shall have the same rights . . . to make and enforce contracts, to sue, be parties, give evidence, and to the full and equal benefit of all laws." Then, in 1868, the 14th Amendment made still deeper inroads in the legal battle to live up to America's ideals. This amendment stated that "all persons born or **naturalized** in the United States . . . are citizens . . . nor shall any State deprive any person of life, liberty, or property, without **due process of law**; nor deny to any person . . . the equal protection of the laws."

These changes to American laws were important steps in the fight against prejudice—but in real life, most black Americans still faced prejudice every day. The Civil Rights Movement of the 1960s continued the struggle, and another major victory was won in 1964, when the Civil Rights Act was passed. It prohibited employment discrimination based on race, sex, national origin, or religion. Part of the act, Title VI, also made public access discrimination against the law. This meant that blacks could no longer be barred from entering the same public buildings as whites—and it led to school **desegregation**. Another part of the Civil Rights Act, Title VIII, was the first federal fair housing law. In other words, landlords and realtors couldn't refuse to let someone rent or buy a house because she was black. This law was added to in 1988, and the Civil Rights Act of 1991 also added to Title VII protections, including the right to a jury trial.

Today, America is doing a much better job at living up to its ideals than it did two hundred years ago, a hundred years ago, or even fifty years ago. Laws are a good way to protect people's rights and fight prejudice.

But ultimately, prejudice is something that lives *inside* people. No law can change the way a person thinks about others. That's something we have to do. We do it by changing the way we talk and act. We do it by changing the way we think.

CELEBRATING DIVERSITY

One of the first things that has to change is the way we think about differences. Instead of being frightened of the ways people are different from ourselves, we need to start feeling curious and interested. We need to be willing to learn from people who are different. We need to enjoy the differences!

Most people enjoy diversity when it comes to the world around them. They like different kinds of food. They read different kinds of books. They enjoy different kinds of music and television shows. The world would be pretty boring if everything was exactly the same!

People are also diverse, in the same way the rest of the world is. Although all of us feel the same basic emotions—sadness and happiness, anger and laughter, loneliness and pride, jealousy and compassion, to name just a few—and most of us have pretty

Each human fingerprint is completely unique. As human beings, we are both all the same and all different from one another.

much the same structure—a head, a body, arms and legs—we also are different in many ways. Our hair, eyes, and skin come in different colors. Our noses are big or little or something in between. Our bodies are different sizes and shapes. And when you get down to the details—to our fingerprints and the DNA inside our cells—we're absolutely unique, despite all the things we have in common with other human beings. Each of us looks at the world a little differently. We believe different things. And we offer different things as well.

The world is a richer place because of all this human diversity. You can learn from and enjoy your friends because, although they're like you in some ways, they're also different from you in other ways. Those differences make them interesting! And in a similar way, we can learn from human beings' different languages, different music, different ways of thinking about God, different lifestyles.

Prejudice, however, focuses on the differences in a negative way. It doesn't value all that differences have to offer us. Instead, it divides people into in-groups and out-groups. It breaks the Golden Rule.

Do you recognize prejudice when you hear it? Sometimes it's hard. We get so used to certain ways of thinking that we

What Is the Golden Rule?

"Treat others the way you want to be treated." It's the most basic of all human moral laws—and it's been found in all religions and all cultures for thousands of years. The earliest record of this principle is in the Code of Hammurabi, written nearly 4,000 years ago. About 2,500 years ago, Confucius, the great Chinese philosopher, wrote, "Never impose on others what you would not choose for yourself." An ancient Egyptian papyrus contains a similar thought: "That which you hate to be done to you, do not do to another." Ancient Greek philosophers wrote, "Do not do to others what would anger you if done to you by others." An early Buddhist teacher expressed a similar concept: "Just as I am so are they, just as they are so am I." Jesus Christ, whom Christians follow, said, "Do unto others as you would have them do unto you." The Prophet Mohammed, whose teachings Muslims follow, said, "As you would have people do to you, do to them; and what you dislike to be done to you, don't do to them," as well as, "That which you seek for yourself, seek for all humans."

You can't follow this ancient rule and practice prejudice. The Golden Rule and prejudice are not compatible!

become blind to what's really going on. But anytime you hear people being lumped together, chances are prejudice is going on. Statements like these are all signs of prejudice:

Poor kids smell bad.
Girls run funny.
Old people are boring.
Special ed kids are weird.
Jocks are jerks.

Rather than building bridges between people, prejudice puts up walls. It makes it hard to talk to others or understand them. And those walls can lead to hatred, violence, and even wars.

A first step to ending prejudice is speaking up against it whenever you hear it. Point it out when you hear your friends or family being prejudiced. They may not even realize that's what they're being.

But even more important, you need to spot prejudice when it's inside you. A recent study of college students, published in *Science Daily*, found that young adults claimed they would be upset by racial remarks against blacks—and yet in reality, the majority either said nothing or made a racial remark of their

Martin Luther King Jr., the great Civil Rights leader, said, "I have a dream that my four little children will one day live in a nation where they will not be judged by the color of their skin but by the content of their character." We can help make his dream come true.

own when confronted with a racial slur against black Americans. None of us wants to think we're prejudiced. It's hard work to recognize the prejudice we ourselves practice. But as Wilhelmina Brown said in the last chapter, we need to "call it by name. And then refuse to act on it. Tie it up and throw it away."

That's not always easy, of course. Here are some ways experts suggest you can fight prejudice when you find it inside yourself:

1. Learn more about groups of people who are different from you. Read books about their history; read fiction that allows you to walk in their shoes in your imagination; watch movies that portray them accurately.

2. Get to know people who are different from you. Practice being a good listener, focusing on what they have to say rather than on your own opinions and experiences. Ask about others' backgrounds and family stories.

3. Practice compassion. Imagine what it would feel like to be someone who is different from you. Your imagination is a powerful tool you can use to make the world better!

Barack Obama, the first black President of the United States, said, "Change will not come if we wait for some other person or some other time. We are the ones we've been waiting for. We are the change that we seek."

4. Believe in yourself. Surprisingly, a lot of the time, psychologists say, prejudice is caused by having a bad self-concept. If you don't like who you are and you don't believe in your own abilities, you're more likely to be scared and threatened by others. People who are comfortable with themselves are also more comfortable with people who are different from themselves.

What does it all come down to in the end? Perhaps the war against prejudice can best be summed up with just two words: communication and respect.

FIND OUT MORE

In Books

Dalton, C. H. *A Practical Guide to Racism.* New York: Gotham, 2008.

Rattansi, Alan. *Racism: A Very Short Introduction.* New York: Oxford University Press, 2007.

Schneider, Dorothy and Carl J. Schneider. *Slavery in America: From Colonial Times to the Civil War: An Eyewitness History.* New York: Facts on File, 2000.

On the Internet

101 WAYS TO COMBAT PREJUDICE
www.uen.org/utahlink/tours/tourFames.cgi?tour_id=15150

BLACK HISTORY
www.blackhistory.com

CIVIL RIGHTS MOVEMENT
www.cnn.com/EVENTS/1997/mlk/links.html

Glossary

abolition: The act of getting rid of something completely.

banished: Thrown out of a country or community.

cystic fibrosis: A lung disease that appears in children.

desegregation: To abolish separating people based on race.

due process of law: Administering justice based on established rules.

effeminate: Have feminine qualities. Usually applied to men in a negative way.

emancipation: The act of setting free.

Enlightenment: A philosophical movement in the 18th century that focused on reason as a way to understand the world.

genes: A unit of heredity passed on from parents to their children.

ideal: What is most perfect.

importation: The act of bringing something into a country from another country.

justification: The act of proving that one's actions are right.

metaphor: Something that symbolizes something else; often used in literature.

migration: The act of moving from one place to another.

naturalized: To make into a citizen.

oversimplification: The act of making something less complicated than it really is.

sickle cell disease: A disease of the blood, in which red blood cells are misshapen.

temperate: Neither too hot nor too cold.

unalienable: Unable to be taken away.

BIBLIOGRAPHY

Farley, John E. *Majority-Minority Relations, 5th ed.* Upper Saddle River, N.J.: Prentice Hall, 2005.

Finkenbine, Roy E. *Source of the African-American Past: Primary Sources in American History.* New York: Longman, 1997.

Hahn, Steven. *A Nation Under Our Feet: Black Struggles in the Rural South, from Slavery to the Great Migration.* Cambridge, Mass.: Belknap Press, 2003.

Henslin, James. *Essentials of Sociology, 6th ed.* Boston: Allyn and Bacon, 2006.

Higginbotham, A. Leon. *In the Matter of Color: The Colonial Period.* New York: Oxford University Press, 1978.

Kolchin, Peter. *American Slavery.* New York: Penguin, 1995.

Meltzer, Milton. *Slavery: From the Rise of Western Civilization to Today.* New York: Dell, 1977.

Schneider, Dorothy and Carl J. Schneider. *Slavery in America: From Colonial Times to the Civil War: An Eyewitness History.* New York: Facts on File, 2000.

ScienceDaily. "Prejudice Could Cost a Black Worker Thousands." Dec. 17, 2008, ww.sciencedaily.com/releases/2008/12/081217124150.htm.

———. "Surprisingly High Tolerance for Racism Revealed." Jan. 8, 2009, www.sciencedaily.com/releases/2009/01/090108144747.htm.

Tannenbaum, Frank. *Slave and Citizen: The Negro in the Americas.* New York: Vintage Books, 1996.

Index

Picture Credits

About the Author

Jaime A. Seba studied political science at Syracuse University before switching her focus to communications. She has worked both in New York and on the West Coast as an activist for LGBT awareness. She is currently a freelance writer based in Seattle.